Henry and Evaline

A Love Under Construction Prequel

PENNY ZELLER

Maplebrook

Cheryl ~
Enjoy Gram's
Story!
Blessings,
Penny Psalm 19:14

Henry and Evaline

Published by Maplebrook Publishing

Editing and copyediting by Mountain Peak Edits and Design
https://mountainpeakedits.com

This novel is a work of fiction. Unless otherwise indicated, all the names, characters, businesses, places, events and incidents in this book are either a figment of the author's imagination or used in a fictitious manner. Any resemblance to actual persons, living or dead, incidents, locales, settings, organizations, businesses, or actual events is purely coincidental. Any brand names or trademarks mentioned throughout are owned by the respective companies.

All scripture quotations are taken from the King James Version of the Bible.

ISBN: 978-0-9760836-5-8

BOOKS BY PENNY ZELLER

Standalone Novels (Maplebrook Publishing)
Love in Disguise

Love in Chokecherry Heights Series (Maplebrook Publishing)
Love Under Construction
Henry and Evaline (novella)

Montana Skies Series (Whitaker House)
McKenzie
Kaydie
Hailee

Love Letters from Ellis Creek Series (Maplebrook Publishing)
Love from Afar

Novella Collections (Barbour)
Love from Afar (The Secret Admirer Romance Collection)
Freedom's Flight (The Underground Railroad Brides Collection)

Nonfiction
77 Ways Your Family Can Make a Difference (Beacon Hill Press)

Children's Fiction
Hollyhocks

To Nanie and Papa, whose love story inspired me to write about true love that lasts for a lifetime.

And we know that all things work together for good to them that love God, to them who are the called according to his purpose. ~ Romans 8:28

CHAPTER ONE

Chokecherry Heights, 1960

Mama, bless her heart, signed Evaline up to be the Bible club helper.

It all happened so fast, Evaline didn't realize the ramifications of Mama's suggestion until it was too late to back out.

They were standing just outside Chokecherry Heights Fellowship with Pastor Gregory's wife, Bessie, who was chatting with Mama, while Dad talked about the sleekest new automobiles with some of the men. Frannie was chit-chatting nonstop as usual, and Great-Grandma was reminding anyone and everyone to feel free to call her by that name.

And Evaline waited patiently, wondering how on earth she was the only non-extroverted person in her family. Not to say she was an introvert, because she wasn't. But she didn't exactly make friends with strangers on a regular basis like the rest of her family did. She likened herself to be somewhere in the middle of outgoing and reserved. Back home in Tennessee, she'd had her group of close friends. Friends she felt comfortable with. Hopefully, she'd make some friends like that here.

She glanced around the parking lot at all the people milling about. She missed her old town 2,000 miles away, but in the two months since her family moved here, Chokecherry Heights was beginning to grow on her.

"Wouldn't you, Evaline?" Mama was saying.

"Pardon?"

"Thank you, Evaline. You will be perfect for the position." Bessie Gregory smiled one of her gracious smiles. Evaline had liked the tall, thin woman with a contagious laugh immediately.

But what had she missed?

"You're right. Evaline will be perfect for the position. She's conscientious, honest, and responsible. And, most importantly, she loves the Lord," Mama said.

"And she's bossy," added Frannie, "So she can keep everyone in line."

Evaline elbowed her younger sister. "What are we talking about, if I might ask?"

"Oh, sorry, dear," said Mama. "I thought you heard us discussing what a wonderful helper you'd make for the new Bible club the church is starting."

"Not that I mind being helpful, but the library position keeps me busy." Evaline loved her job at the Chokecherry Heights Public Library—checking out books, checking in books, cataloging books, and being the first to read the new books when they arrived.

Mama knitted her brows together. "It's not during the day, dear. It's only Wednesday evenings."

"Ooh, neato! I cannot wait for it," exclaimed Frannie. She grabbed Evaline's arm and nearly cut off the circulation in her excitement. "I have been wanting to make new friends this summer before school starts. This might just be my chance. Say you'll do it, Evaline, please?"

Frannie's large hazel eyes peered into Evaline's soul, begging for her to see things Frannie's way. "All right. But what does it entail?"

"Oh, thank you, Evaline. You're a swell sister."

Mrs. Gregory clasped Evaline's hands. "Thank you for serving youth in this way. It's not a difficult job, but it does take commitment. Your most important job will be providing prayer support for the girls. You'll also prepare the treat donation list, hand out the treats, wipe off tables and clean up after the meetings, and be a chaperone on any outings. You'll work with our son, Henry, who is leading the club." Mrs. Gregory paused. "Does this sound like something you'd be interested in?"

Three pairs of eyes bored into her. Frannie leaned closer. "Do it, Evaline, please?"

"All right. I accept the position."

Evaline had never met Henry, but she hoped he was an easy fellow to work with.

***

Henry Gregory climbed into his 1947 red pickup truck and started the engine. It had been a long, but good day. And it would get even better when he joined his parents for dinner. Mom said steak and potatoes were on the menu. His mouth watered at the thought.

A year ago, he moved from home and now rented a one-bedroom house less than a mile from the church for $50 per month, plus upkeep of the place. Not that he minded mowing the lawn and keeping the place tidy. And he wasn't there much anyway. With his job working for Handyman Morales, time spent at his parents' house, church, and soon the Bible club, Henry had just enough time to eat and sleep at the place he now called home.

Drumming his fingers on the steering wheel, Henry thought about the day's events. The Lord had led him to guide the youth at the new Bible club as a part-time volunteer pastor, and things were beginning to fall into place. In three days, he'd lead the first meeting.

When he dedicated his life to Jesus at the age of thirteen, Henry felt the nudge of the Lord to do what he could to assist other youths in making the life-changing choice. Working as the leader for the newly-established Bible club would enable him to make a difference.

Henry sat at his kitchen table and perused, as he had for the past several days, the advertisement in the *Chokecherry Heights Gazette.*

Two-thousand-square-foot shop for sale. Includes small office. Lots of potential.

The advertisement included a photograph of the shop and a number to call to inquire about the property. It would be good to talk with Dad about his plans tonight and get input. Henry prayed that if it was the Lord's will, he would be able to purchase it and use it for his dream. He closed his eyes and once again envisioned the sign he'd place on the outside of the building: *Gregory Home Remodeling*.

Someday, he would expand to also build homes. But in the meantime, he'd take the knowledge he accumulated at his job and remodel homes to the owners' specifications.

At twenty-two years old, Henry knew it was a long road uphill to achieve his goal.

But a challenge never stopped him before.

CHAPTER TWO

The day arrived all too soon.

Evaline climbed behind the wheel of the family car and Frannie plopped into the passenger side. They decided at the last minute to drive to their first Bible club meeting, rather than walk the short distance to the church.

"Ooh, hurry, Evaline. I don't want to be late."

"We'll be on time, Frannie, don't worry."

But her sister wasn't deterred. "I just can't wait to make some new friends. This move has been hard, especially since I had to leave all that I ever knew just before my senior year."

Frannie was far too dramatic. "It'll all work out, you'll see. Besides, it wasn't Dad's fault he lost his job and we had to relocate halfway across the country."

"I know that, but still, it's been hard, leaving my old life behind and picking up and starting all over again. At least you had the choice whether you wanted to stay or move here."

"True. Especially since I'm twenty and no longer in school. I wouldn't have wanted to stay in Tennessee anyhow. I'd miss my family too much."

Frannie peered out the window. "How many kids do you think will be there?"

"No way to tell, but we'll know soon enough."

"Does my hair look all right?"

Evaline rolled her eyes. Frannie always worried about her hair. "It looks fine. Try having a poofy mess like mine." How she wished she had her sister's gorgeous naturally-platinum locks shaped into a perfect bouffant. Frannie's hair, smooth and obedient, was so unlike Evaline's dark blonde bland hair with an overabundance of curls that refused to cooperate.

"At least you have Mama's and Great-Grandma's sparkly blue eyes. Mine are a drab hazel."

Frannie had a point. There was no mistaking Evaline was the daughter of Mama and the great-granddaughter of Great-Grandma.

With five minutes to spare, Evaline pulled the car into a parking spot at Chokecherry Heights Fellowship. The square-shaped white church with a prominent cross and its cranberry-colored front doors beckoned. She took a deep breath. Frannie was by far more excited about this excursion than she was. "Well, here goes nothing," she said.

Her sister bolted through the front doors of the church before Evaline had a chance to exit the automobile. She wished she had Frannie's exuberant personality when it came to meeting people for the first time.

Climbing the nine stairs to the front door, Evaline paused, said a prayer, and took another deep breath before entering the church.

"There you are, dear," greeted Mrs. Gregory. "The cookies are in the kitchen. The Bible club is meeting in the room just adjacent to the kitchen. If you have any questions at all, feel free to ask Henry or I'll be in the sanctuary practicing the piano music for Sunday's services."

Evaline found the plates of cookies just as Mrs. Gregory mentioned. Should she ask Henry Gregory if there was anything she needed to do beforehand? She'd never met the man, although she had seen him speaking with the pastor at church on Sunday. She paced the kitchen for a few minutes, praying and debating about what she ought to do.

Just when Evaline was about to ask if she should join in the meeting and assist where needed, a quick answer to prayer arrived.

"Hello, there."

She turned to see Henry Gregory standing in the kitchen doorway. "We're about to begin. Would you care to join us?"

Evaline followed Mr. Gregory and sat down beside Frannie. An expedient perusal told her there were about fourteen participants. She mentally calculated how many cookies she'd seen on each plate and figured there were more than enough.

"Before we begin, let's go around the tables and introduce each other," suggested Mr. Gregory. "I'll start first. My name is Henry Gregory, but feel free to call me 'Henry'. It'll eliminate confusion since my dad is Pastor Gregory. I have lived in Chokecherry Heights most of my life and enjoy working with wood and playing baseball and basketball." He paused. "We'll start at this table and work our way to the other two tables," he said, pointing at the table where Evaline sat with Frannie and three other teens. Tell us your name, your favorite hobby, and what grade you'll be in when school starts in a couple of months."

It would be beneficial to know everyone's name, Evaline figured, especially since Frannie would likely tell her all about the other teenagers' antics on the way home. Antics Evaline would miss because she was busy with being a Bible club volunteer.

"And your name?" Henry asked, facing her.

"Evaline Browning."

Frannie chose that moment to provide commentary. "But you can call her just 'Evaline', actually, 'Evaline Junior'. She's named after Great-Grandma."

Evaline elbowed Frannie. "You're only a 'junior' if you're a man and named after your father."

Henry chuckled. "'Evaline Junior'. It has a ring to it." If he was attempting to lighten the mood of the participants, it worked, as a loud round of laughter filled the room. If he was attempting to lighten Evaline's mood, he failed. *Thanks, Frannie.*

"And your favorite hobbies?"

His next question brought her back from her inward chastisement of her younger sister. She might as well share so the kids felt more comfortable with her. "I enjoy reading…"

"And more reading."

Several teens laughed at Frannie, the comedian's, interruption.

"Anything else you like to do?"

"I like to sew, listen to my 45s, and go with friends to the soda fountain."

"And drink sweet tea," Frannie volunteered.

Maybe she should just hire Frannie to be her spokeswoman.

"And what grade will you be in this school year?" asked Henry.

"What grade?" Evaline attempted to see if Henry was joshing her, but his expression remained serious.

Frannie smirked.

"Yes, what grade will you be in?"

"I'm not sure…"

An unknown voice in the audience chirped, "Did you hear that? She's not sure."

"She's a hoot," said another.

Henry's eyes crinkled at the corners, and he flashed her an amused grin. "Will you be attending the local high school this fall?"

"No." Evaline wrinkled her nose. She hadn't been in school for over two years. "Wait. You don't think…"

Frannie burst out in an all-out chortle. "Evaline isn't in school. She already graduated."

"She has?" Henry asked. "I'm sorry, Evaline. I had no way of knowing."

"For goodness, y'all. I'm nearly twenty-one years old." Her statement came out as more of a frustrated huff than a gracious statement, and Evaline tempered herself. It wouldn't do to set a poor example.

"My apologies," said Henry, but a teasing glint remained in his eyes.

"Evaline is the Bible club helper," offered Frannie. "Surely Mrs. Gregory told you."

"Actually, yes, she did tell me I would have a helper, but she didn't mention the name. I do apologize, Evaline."

The heat crept up her face. Never again would she let Mama talk her into something.

CHAPTER THREE

Henry pushed the rotary lawn mower through the grass. The necessary, but somewhat mundane, chore gave him time to think. The first night of the Bible club had gone well, with the exception of his blunder in mistaking Evaline Browning for a student. Where had his brain been?

He'd done a skillful job of hiding his own embarrassment, but poor Evaline Browning. Her pretty face blushed when he made what she would likely consider a grievous error. Her facial expression and response said it all, although he could tell she attempted to hide her horror at being seen as a youth.

With her sitting at the table with the other students, combined with her petite frame and youthful appearance, how could he think she was anything but one of the participants?

Henry finished mowing, then headed into the house to shower and go to dinner at his parents' house. He opened his bureau drawer, specifically searching for the comfortable zip-down pullover shirt with the green-striped collar that he hadn't worn in a while. As he pilfered, he came to the bottom of the drawer and pulled out the shirt. But not before a wrinkled photograph caught his eye.

He rarely thought about the photograph, but upon seeing it today, it brought about a slew of emotions. A lump formed in his throat as he stared at his five-year-old self. Eyes sad, shoulders slumped, unkempt hair, and holes in the knees of his trousers. An alcoholic father and a neglectful mother made for a difficult childhood.

The day seemed like yesterday. Henry was crouched in the corner of his room. His dad's drunken rages frightened him, and for good reason. Even at his tender age, he knew no child deserved to be hit.

Would Daddy come back in and be mad at him again? He'd tried not to do anything wrong.

His tummy growled. He was so hungry. Why did Mommy always forget to feed him? She only came home once in a while. Would she be back tonight?

A squeal of brakes sounded outside, and Henry removed his arms protectively covering his head and ran into the front room to peer out the window.

His aunt and uncle's dark blue sedan lurched to a stop and Uncle Quinn stepped from the vehicle in a hurry. Henry's dad started toward him, his hands in fists.

Would Daddy hurt Uncle Quinn like he had hurt Henry?

Henry hoped not. He really liked his uncle.

Aunt Bessie stared out the sedan window. She appeared frightened too.

A loud commotion took place then, and Henry's body stiffened. What would happen?

"Where is Henry?" his uncle asked.

His dad let out a slew of words Henry knew not to repeat.

Uncle Quinn stood face to face with Daddy and Henry shivered at the exchanged words. He wanted to tell his uncle he was in the house and wanted to run to the sedan and climb into it with Aunt Bessie. She'd always been so kind to him.

But instead his feet remained planted on the filthy floor.

His uncle shoved past his dad and stalked into the house. "Henry?" he asked.

Henry recalled the calm way his uncle said his name. His voice when he spoke to Henry was always so gentle, not like his dad's harsh voice.

He ran to Uncle Quinn and wrapped his arms around his leg. "Take me with you," he begged.

"We are."

Henry remembered wondering if he'd heard correctly or if maybe his aunt and uncle were taking him only for a visit.

He didn't want to just visit. He wanted to stay with them.

"You ain't taking him nowhere," his dad yelled. He shoved Henry aside, raised a fist, and hit Uncle Quinn.

Henry cowered against the wall and held up his hands to cover his eyes. But he wanted to see what would happen next, so he peeked between two of his fingers. Would Uncle Quinn be all right? He held his breath.

Uncle Quinn came toward his dad and held up a fist. "You deserve a pummeling," he snarled. His eye then caught Henry's, and he lowered his fist. "But I won't."

Then his uncle spoke again to his dad. "We are taking Henry and we aren't bringing him back."

Could Henry have heard correctly? Dare he hope?

"Son, go get your things and meet Aunt Bessie in the car," said Uncle Quinn.

Henry needn't be told twice. He scurried to his room and grabbed his other shirt and a wrinkled photograph, his only possessions.

In the front room, the two adults exchanged more words, only this time in quieter tones. "Go ahead, son," said Uncle Quinn, pointing to the door.

Aunt Bessie now stood beside the car, and he ran to her waiting arms. She kneeled to his height, and he could see she'd been crying. "We love you, Henry Gregory," she said, and planted a kiss on his forehead. "And you are coming with us forever."

"You ain't bringing me back?"

"We're not bringing you back."

"For sure?"

"For sure, Henry."

Could it be true? He glanced around to see if his mom had returned. But she hadn't. Would she know he was gone?

His aunt and uncle legally adopted him and made him theirs. Henry never again saw either of his former parents.

On that day, Henry never again called them "aunt" and "uncle". They became "mom" and "dad".

Uncle Quinn became his hero and Aunt Bessie the caring mother he never had.

And Henry never looked back except on rare occasions like today, and on those days, he was reminded of God's goodness and how He was the giver of second chances, a Father who redeemed what had been lost and restored what was broken.

***

Dinner at his parents' house was always the highlight of any day for Henry.

After eating two helpings of Mom's lasagna, the three retreated to the porch. "How did the first Bible club meeting go?" Dad asked.

"It went well with the exception of me accidentally mistaking Evaline Browning for one of the youths."

"I can see how one might do that, as she's petite and looks younger than her years."

"Which she will appreciate when she gets older," added Mom.

Henry shook his head. "She didn't appreciate it now."

"I'm sure she'll forgive you. She seems like such a sweet girl. The entire family is just delightful." Mom sipped on her lemonade. "Don't you think she seems like a sweet girl?" A gleam in her eyes caused suspicion.

"Considering we got off on the wrong foot…"

Dad chuckled. "Her great-grandmother is a card. She insisted everyone call her Great-Grandma the first time we met her."

"I remember that," said Mom. "I called her Mrs. Vaughn, but she would have none of it. Said everyone considered her their great-grandma anyway, so just to call her that."

They shared another round of laughs before sitting in comfortable silence and taking in the pleasant early-June evening. The rediscovery of the photograph remained faintly in his mind. As he observed Dad, he pondered how he could be so different from Henry's biological father, even though they were brothers. They both shared the same hair color, but that was where the resemblance ended, both in appearance and character.

When Henry was younger, he couldn't fathom that a God with so many day-to-day items to tend to and so many people to take care of, had seen to it to rescue Henry. When he'd learned that God even cared for the sparrows, the realization impacted him. Now, years later, and having grown significantly in his faith, Henry knew.

"How are the sermons coming?" Dad asked, interrupting Henry's thoughts.

"I have a new appreciation for pastors. It takes a lot of time and prayer to make sure the message is delivered accurately."

"That it does. You're speaking into the lives of teenagers and making a difference for eternity."

The words sunk deep inside Henry's soul. He had a heart for reaching youth with the Gospel. He only hoped he could do it adequately.

Mom reached over and patted him on the arm. "You know leading the Bible club is entirely your decision."

"We don't want you to feel obligated just because you're a pastor's son," added Dad.

"Oh, I don't feel obligated. And thank you, Mom. I know it is my decision, and one I don't take lightly. I want to lead the Bible club; I just hope I can do it effectively."

Mom's eyes misted. "We have no doubt you can do it effectively. Lift it up in prayer and God will guide you. We are so proud of you, Henry."

Mom had never missed a chance to let him know she and Dad were proud of him. How had he been so fortunate to be their son?

"On another note, have you called yet on the building?" asked Dad.

"Not yet. I'm still praying about that. I know I'll have to start small at first, and I don't want to be so busy that I lack sufficient time for the Bible club."

"Sounds like you've given this a lot of thought, and you're right about wanting to keep your priorities in order, which isn't always easy." Dad paused. "If you need anything, you know where to turn."

"Thanks, Dad."

Now if only Henry could work up the courage to take the next step toward his dream.

CHAPTER FOUR

After church, Evaline's family gathered around a table for the after-church potluck. Because it was raining outside, the congregants met in the same room where the Bible club meeting was held.

Evaline sandwiched herself between Frannie and Great-Grandma and awaited her turn to stand in line for the meal. Mama sat between Dad and Great-Grandma.

"Ooh, there's that cute boy I was telling you about," Frannie whispered, nearly leaping out of her seat. "Do you see him over there? The one with the really dark hair? He was at the Bible club meeting. I think his name is Kenny."

Frannie was far too hyper. Evaline followed her sister's gaze to a table across the room. "Do you see him?" repeated Frannie.

"What are y'all talking about?" Great-Grandma asked, leaning forward for a better chance of hearing the conversation.

Fortunately for Frannie, Great-Grandma's question wasn't answered because it was Evaline's family's turn to stand in line. Once at the table with the mounds of food, Evaline helped herself to some casserole and a deviled egg. Next, she came upon a bowl of purple and green grapes someone had graciously removed from the vines. She scooped a portion with the oversized stainless steel spoon.

Her gaze settled on Henry, who stood across the table from her.

Returning her attention to the food, Evaline attempted to place the heap of grapes onto her plate. All was well until Frannie decided at just that moment to run into the back of her, likely due to inattention or because she was staring at that Kenny boy. The pile of grapes spilled and one landed on Henry's plate. Right in the middle of his potato salad.

"Oh, oops," quipped Frannie. "I wasn't paying attention."

"Sorry," said Evaline.

Henry had the grace to smile and pluck the grape from his potato salad. "Would you like it back?" he asked.

She attempted to utter a simple "no thank you," but the words wouldn't come.

Why was she so nervous around him?

He stared at her, probably hoping for an answer. Instead, Evaline busied herself with placing more grapes on her plate and arranging them in a circle. Maybe if she avoided eye contact he would forget about the entire incident.

Finally, after what seemed like an hour, the line moved, and Evaline found her way back to her family's table.

Sometime later, Pastor Gregory stood in the front of the room.

"Hello, everyone. It's so nice to see you all here today. I hope you are enjoying the delicious meal. I have a few announcements." His pleasant smile seemed to individually connect with each of those in attendance. "First of all, our board of elders has voted unanimously to expand the church building. As you know, Chokecherry Heights Fellowship has been growing in recent months. Secondly, for those of you who don't know him, I would like to introduce my son, Henry Gregory. Henry, would you please come up to the front?"

Henry stood from his seat at a table somewhere behind Evaline and joined his father. "As we announced last Sunday, Henry is in charge of the new Bible club ministry for youth. We saw a need for such a club here in Chokecherry Heights, and have opened it, not only to the young people in our church, but also to those in the community. If you have a son or daughter who is interested in fellowship with other youth, please bring them to the Bible club on Wednesday evenings at 6:00 p.m." Several murmurs filled the room, and Evaline figured there would be even more teenagers at the next meeting.

Pastor Gregory continued. "Henry, can you tell us a bit about how that's going?"

Evaline watched as Henry lengthened his posture and stood up even taller. So the man was handsome in a Ricky Nelson sort of way. She'd give him that. But there was something beneath that handsome and cordial exterior just emanating mystery. Much like the mysteries on the shelves at the library.

"Thank you, Dad. We had fourteen youth at the Bible club last Wednesday, and I'm expecting it to grow. Ten were from our church. I'm excited to see what the Lord does with this ministry."

"Excellent. Can you tell us about your upcoming plans for the club?"

Henry nodded. "Yes. Next Saturday, we are planning to do a service project. As a matter of fact, I'd like to include the youth in a service project once a month on Saturdays. We can start with the needs of our church body and expand into the community."

"He is such an eloquent speaker," Great-Grandma said a little too loudly. "Don't you think he's an eloquent speaker, Evaline?"

While she loved Great-Grandma with all her being, was named after her, and even resembled Great-Grandma in her younger years, there was one thing Evaline would not take after Great-Grandma in, and that was in her meddlesome ways. The woman was

37

what people called a "matchmaker". Such a title held no appeal for Evaline.

Meanwhile, at the front of the room, Pastor Gregory continued his discussion with Henry.

"I really like that idea. Being Jesus's hands and feet is so critical to our witness. If anyone has a service project need, please see Henry after the potluck so he can add you to the list." He paused. "Thank you, Henry. Will you keep us updated in the coming months?"

"Yes, sir, I definitely will."

Henry took his seat again while the people in the room clapped.

"I think that's all for announcements. Please partake in this bounty of food and be sure to have seconds, as there is plenty."

Great-Grandma chose that exact moment to interject. She waved her hand in the air. "Pastor?"

Evaline nudged Frannie. "Oh, no," she mouthed. There was no telling what she could be up to this time.

"Yes, Mrs….er, Great-Grandma."

Great-Grandma stood and steadied herself by clutching the table. "That is all so marvelous about the young Mr. Gregory. However, you forgot something very important."

"What is that?" asked Pastor Gregory.

"You forgot that our dear Evaline is the Bible club helper."

Evaline wanted to die on the spot. "I bequeath to you my books, clothes, and 45s," she whispered to Frannie. All eyes focused on her. If dying on the spot wasn't possible, maybe she could crawl under the table. She squirmed in her chair and did her best to ignore Frannie's snickers. The heat crept up her face and she feared what might come next.

Pastor Gregory grinned. "I am so sorry about that. Evaline, would you care to come up front and tell us how your first week went as the Bible club helper?"

I'd rather not.

Mama nodded toward the front of the room. Frannie snickered again. Dad shook his head and chuckled. And Great-Grandma patted her on the arm. "Well, go ahead, dear. You're somewhat of a celebrity in our family now."

Evaline teetered on shaky legs, as all eyes in the congregation peered at her. She smoothed the wrinkles in her skirt and nearly tripped over nothing as she walked toward the front of the room.

"Church friends, this is Evaline Browning. She and her family moved here a couple of months ago. She volunteered to assist Henry with the Bible club. Tell us, Evaline, how did the first week go?"

Well, for one, I didn't volunteer. It was Mama who volunteered me…

Speaking in front of crowds always made Evaline nervous. Hence the reason she attempted to avoid reading to the children during the library's story time. She swallowed, closed her eyes, swallowed again, shifted from one foot to the other, prayed she wouldn't pass out, then addressed the crowd.

"I—it's going swell."

"And what exactly do you do, Evaline?" Pastor Gregory asked.

"I—I am a mentor and I pray with the young women, pass out treats, wipe off tables and clean up, and when we do the service projects, I will be a chaperone." Her voice sounded shaky in her own ears and she inwardly cringed.

"We are thankful for your generous spirit. Thank you for volunteering."

Henry grinned at her and she forgot who she was and where she was.

And because Evaline couldn't move her feet, she remained planted. Everyone in the room began to clap. Seconds turned into minutes. Minutes turned into…

"Evaline?" asked Pastor Gregory.

"Yes?"

"You may return to your seat now if you'd like."

CHAPTER FIVE

Evaline peered through the doorway and counted the number of participants in tonight's Bible club. Sixteen. Unwrapping the plates of chocolate-frosted cupcakes one of the church members donated, she counted and came up short. That would never do, and she knew she needed to find Mrs. Gregory and inquire as to whether there were more treats. Evaline left the kitchen and headed toward the front of the sanctuary where the pastor's wife was arranging a lovely display of fake flowers.

"I thought there were three plates, but let's check," she said, leading Evaline to her car in the parking lot. "Mrs. Tidwell's son carried them in for me before he mowed the church lawn." Sure enough, a plate of vanilla-frosted cupcakes remained on the car seat.

"That's a relief," said Evaline. "We were short a few. This will be just enough."

Carrying the additional plate to the kitchen, Evaline unwrapped those as well, and just in time to hand them out to the club members. It was as she distributed the cupcakes that she noticed something unsettling.

Someone had taken a bite out of one of the chocolate-frosted cupcakes.

"Ooh, someone sampled that one," said Frannie, instead reaching for one with vanilla frosting.

When she approached Henry, only the partially-eaten cupcake remained.

His eyebrows lifted into his hairline. "What happened to this one?"

"I'm sorry, but it's the only one left."

Snickers arose from the group. "I suppose we should have a brief lesson on patience, as someone obviously didn't exhibit patience." He lifted it from the plate and peered at the teeth marks in the frosting. "Are you the one who took a bite, Evaline?"

"No, I'm not fond of cupcakes."

Frannie chose that moment to voice her thoughts. "Now, if it was chocolate chip cookies, you would have a suspect for sure. She would be five-foot-two, curly dark blonde hair, blue eyes, Southern accent…"

Several of the students laughed at Frannie's description of Evaline. "Very funny," Evaline retorted. "Besides, I would not have taken just a bite of the cookie, I would have eaten the entire thing."

Henry's throaty laugh at her comment was contagious, and those in the group joined in. "We'll know not to suggest chocolate chip cookies for the snack," he said. "But that doesn't solve the mystery. Any ideas?"

It was then that Evaline peered up at him. Was that a smidge of chocolate frosting near the dimple in his cheek? "Might it have been you, Henry?" she asked.

A glint lit his blue-gray eyes. "Suppose I could come clean about the actual topic of discussion. Students, we'll be talking about how, even though we might think we are getting away with something, God always knows the truth."

Evaline couldn't hide her amusement at his witty response. While he came across as quiet, Henry Gregory certainly had an ornery streak.

***

On Saturday morning, everyone met at the home of Mr. and Mrs. Kafka. Henry's prayers for a clear day and a favorable turnout had been answered. Eight youth showed up ready to make a difference for the couple who had recently struggled with a multitude of health issues.

"Hello, everyone. Thank you for coming. The Kafkas have a vast yard with many opportunities for cleanup. The shovels, rakes, mower, and other tools are near the shed in the corner." Henry opened them with a word of prayer before they began working.

Sometime later, he approached Evaline, who was busy weeding the garden. "Do you have a minute?" he asked.

Evaline stood and dusted off her pedal pushers. She was adorably disheveled with her tousled hair and some dried mud on her nose. The more he was around her, the more he was drawn to her.

Interesting since he'd just met her.

"Everyone is working really hard," she said.

"That they are. This will greatly benefit Mr. and Mrs. Kafka. Mom mentioned the church ladies have started a meal train. The men's group has been looking for a new vehicle to replace the couple's old car that no longer runs so they can get to and from doctor's appointments." Henry paused. "Don't let on I told you about the car. It's going to be a surprise."

"My lips are sealed."

Something stirred in him about how easily he and Evaline undertook ministry opportunities together.

They stood in silence for a few moments before Henry brought up the topic on his mind. "May I tell you something in confidence?"

"Absolutely."

"Are you familiar with Roberta and Ray Orlov's situation?"

Evaline tilted her head to one side. "Situation?"

Henry chewed on the inside of his cheek. This was the part of ministry that proved difficult. "Their father is struggling with alcoholism."

Evaline raised her brows. "Really? I know Roberta asked for prayer at the last Bible club meeting, but she wouldn't elaborate. She just said that since God was all-knowing, He would know what her concern was, and she asked for us to pray for that concern."

"Will you join me in continuing to pray for them and for wisdom as we come alongside them in their time of need?"

"Yes, Henry. Yes, I will."

"Thank you. As you know, their family attends our church, and I imagine my dad and the elders will want to do all they can to assist as well."

"God has placed us in Roberta and Ray's path for a reason."

As they stood discussing Roberta and Ray's situation, Henry knew that God had also placed Evaline in his path for a reason.

***

Henry returned to work trimming the trees. His blue-gray eyes had taken on a somber expression and for a moment, his attention seemed miles away during their conversation.

She admired his servant's heart and his concern for others. She made a note to pray for, not only Roberta,

Ray, and their family, but also for Henry, that he would have wisdom in handling this matter.

"Hey, everyone!" Kenny exclaimed. "How about we have us a game of tag?"

There wasn't time for a general consensus because Frannie nominated herself as the first tagger. She was a fast one and tagged her victim in a few seconds.

Evaline had never been much of a runner, so when Henry tagged her on the arm after less than five seconds of chasing her around the yard, it came as no surprise. "You're it," he said. His touch caused a jolt to zip up her arm.

She shrugged off the realization that Henry had an effect on her. Temporarily.

Finally, sometime later, Henry made an announcement. "Thank you, everyone, for coming today. You can leave the tools against the side of the shed, and I'll retrieve them later. For now, let's go to the soda fountain."

Cheers and applause erupted, as the teenagers climbed into the back of Henry's truck. "Evaline, care to join me in the cab?" he asked.

It was much preferred to cramming into the back, so Evaline agreed. As they rode to the soda fountain, Evaline caught a glimpse of Henry's profile. His strong jawline and ruffled brown hair added to his rugged appearance. An appearance that some girls would find attractive. Some girls, like Evaline.

But she would keep that little morsel of information to herself.

CHAPTER SIX

Evaline felt most at home in the library. If she had her druthers, she'd build an enormous room with floor-to-ceiling shelves full of books. Moveable stairs would enable her to reach the top shelves. And in the corner of the enormous room would be a comfy sofa with plump pillows where she'd lounge and read the latest mystery novel. While mystery novels were her favorite, there was plenty of room in her life for all genres.

Slipping into a daydream, she envisioned the room. Shiny wood flooring, a world map spanning an entire wall, a fresh bouquet of flowers on a desk with a typewriter, and a huge pitcher of unlimited sweet tea. At last count, she'd have 4,000 books on the shelves, all begging to be read. A smile lit her face. She could stay there forever.

"Excuse me, Evaline, Junior?"

Evaline returned to real life to see Henry standing across from the counter. "Oh, hello. And it's just 'Evaline'," she said, trying not to fumble her words.

He quirked a brow at her and a slow grin crossed his face.

"May I help you?" she squeaked. Surely Henry could have arrived at the library at any other time than when she was stuck in a pleasant daydream.

Still grinning, he plopped a sizeable stack of books on the counter. "I'd like to check out these books."

"Sure." She started with the top book about building with wood and removed the card from the pocket and handed it to him for his signature. She then stamped both the card and the due date slip. She continued to the next several books, all on woodworking, until she reached the final book. "*How to Crochet a Blanket in Three Easy Steps?*" she asked. Her eyes met his. "Do you crochet?"

He nodded. "As a matter of fact, I hope to enter a blanket in the Chokecherry Heights fair this fall."

"Really?"

She hadn't expected him to be the sewing type.

Henry chuckled, his amusement echoing through the library until Mrs. Gowrie, who was returning books to their rightful places on the shelves hissed, "ssh!"

He leaned toward her and whispered. "I was just joshing you, Evaline. I'm not really hoping to learn to crochet and I won't be entering a blanket in the fair."

"Then why did you want to check out this book?"

His smirk said it all.

Why was the man so utterly ornery?

***

Finally, Friday arrived. Some weeks seemed longer than others, and such was the case for this week. Evaline had extra duties at the library, including having to read to the children because the regular librarian was out sick.

She was about to slip into something more comfortable when Frannie halted her in her tracks. "Best not change out of your skirt."

"Why is that?"

"I overheard Mama and Great-Grandma talking about us having a guest tonight."

Before Evaline could ask who the guest was, the doorbell rang.

"Sounds like the guest is here," said Frannie, always the alert one.

Evaline ran a brush through her hair, which was overly humidified today due to the rain. Catching a glimpse of herself in the mirror, she gaped in horror at the frizzy mess. There really was no hope for curls infused with humidity. If only she could have been born with Frannie's hair. She sighed.

Some things in life were so unfair.

The guest was probably someone from Dad's work at Chokecherry Heights Co-op or one of Mama's friends from church. They wouldn't be concerned with Evaline's constant dilemma with her hair.

She pressed the wrinkles from her blouse, tucked it in to her skirt, and left the room she shared with Frannie. Weariness beckoned her and she longed for a bubble bath and a good night's rest. Hopefully, whoever the guest was wasn't the chatty sort.

"Oh, Evaline, there you are," said Great-Grandma. "Guess who I invited to dinner?"

Evaline really had no idea, as it could any number of new friends her family had made during their short stint in Chokecherry Heights. "Who?" she asked.

Great-Grandma's lack of eye contact caused Evaline's suspicions to rise.

"Where is the guest?" she asked.

"He went outside for a moment with your dad to look at something in the garage." Great-Grandma ambled toward her. "There now, Evaline, let's do something with that hair." She reached forward and pressed Evaline's fluffy curls against her head. "You poor dear. You didn't only inherit my name and blue eyes, but also my hair."

Evaline did not need to be reminded of that fact.

Great-Grandma slowly stepped back from her. "Well, that's the best we can do. Now then, why don't you join your mother in preparing the meal?"

Before Evaline could do so, the door opened and the surprise of all surprises entered.

"Henry?" she asked.

Great-Grandma chortled. "Well, of course. Who did y'all think tonight's special guest was? The president?"

Evaline hadn't expected it to be Henry.

"Hi, Evaline."

"Dinner's almost ready," Mama announced.

Evaline scampered away to join Mama and Frannie in the kitchen. "How come no one told me Henry was coming for dinner?"

"Didn't think it mattered," shrugged Frannie. "Remember, in Tennessee we had dinner guests all the time. Gonna be the same here."

"But the guests weren't…"

"Someone you might like?"

"Evaline," said Mama, "I'm sorry you weren't warned. I didn't realize Great-Grandma hadn't told you she invited him."

At least Mama understood Evaline's plight. Was there time to find a mirror and do something about her wayward curls?

***

Everyone sat down at the table for dinner. Henry had been nervous at first to visit the Browning home. Sure, he'd met Evaline, Frannie, and Great-Grandma, but had not formally met Evaline's parents. However, Mr. Browning set Henry at ease the moment they stepped outside and he and Mr. Browning chatted for a few minutes about wood and building things. Then Henry assisted him in bringing in a new piece of furniture for the front room.

An unpleasant food odor lingered in the air, and Henry attempted to hide his awareness of the pungent stench. What on earth was for dinner?

Great-Grandma directed traffic and situated him right next to Evaline. He didn't know who was more embarrassed: Evaline or himself.

After Mr. Browning said grace, a huge pan was passed around the table. Henry eyed the unknown food and debated whether or not to place some of its contents on his plate. On one hand, it was the polite thing to do. On the other hand, he wasn't sure what it was. He regarded the green vegetable-like substance in the pan and his gag reflex responded. At least there were what appeared to be onions and perhaps some little ham pieces mixed in. That might make it more palatable.

Not that he ever wanted to complain about food. He knew what it was like to do without. But the mystery vegetable... he struggled to maintain a neutral facial expression. While he ate carrots, potatoes, broccoli, romaine lettuce, and peas on a regular basis, he'd never eaten this before. He was sure of it.

Great-Grandma, who was sure to sit on his left-hand side, leaned toward him. "Those are collard greens with ham. They've been a favorite of our family for generations. Old recipe passed down." She waited for his response, her blue eyes expectant beneath cat-eye glasses. "Go ahead, Henry, try some. You can't very well expect to be a member of this family if you don't cotton to collard greens."

Henry wanted to tell her that since he wasn't a member of the family, although it was a nice gesture, he likely wouldn't "cotton" to the collard greens anytime soon. They reminded him of old spinach left in a bowl of water and forgotten about for several days. His stomach growled and he longed for some lasagna or steak and potatoes.

But politeness won the war waging within him, and Henry scooped out a meager portion onto his plate. It made a "slopping" noise, and the gag reflex returned.

"You need more than that, Henry. You'll starve to death. Can't have you all malnourished." Great-

Grandma took her own spoon and spooned several helpings onto his plate. "Granted, I'm originally from Chokecherry Heights, but I did a long enough stint in Tennessee to become quite fond of collard greens and ham. Besides, there are dandelion greens in there all mixed in, making the dish all the more delectable."

"And Evaline made the cornbread. You really must try the cornbread," Frannie informed him, as she passed the pan his way.

Now cornbread was something he could easily live with. As a matter of fact, there was no reason why he couldn't live on cornbread alone for this meal. Henry put a piece on his plate and slathered it with some butter.

"The cornbread looks delicious, Evaline," he said, turning to her. A rosy blush covered her face.

She was extra cute when that happened.

"Thank you, Henry."

"Well, goodness," said Great-Grandma, interrupting his thoughts about Evaline. "I'm so thankful, Henry, that you and Evaline have thrown formalities to the wayside and are not calling each other 'miss this' and 'mister that'. Since y'all are working together, it's only proper. Besides, the sound of the names Henry and Evaline all in one sentence have a charming ring to them, if I do say so myself."

Henry reined in his embarrassment. Great-Grandma was so presumptuous. Mr. Browning cleared his throat. Mrs. Browning covered her mouth with her hand. Frannie laughed, and Evaline muttered an anguished "oh, y'all".

Mrs. Browning had mercy on he and Evaline and changed the subject.

"I understand you work for Handyman Morales," she said.

"I do. I really like working with wood." Henry devoured his cornbread. Would Mom approve of his decision to reach for another piece before eating the main meal? *If I ever do eat the main meal.* Growing up, Mom constantly reinforced the importance of being a gentleman and possessing respectable table manners. Would the fact he was feeling undernourished be a justifiable reason to have an emergency second helping of cornbread?

The conversation around him continued while Henry faced his king-sized decision. Was that potato salad across the table? Maybe he could live on that and cornbread.

Great-Grandma backed him further into the proverbial corner. "Now, Henry. You really must try the collard greens. While you are far from being a puny boy, you still need your vegetables, what with working two jobs and all. Besides, there's homemade pecan pie for dessert. Evaline loves collard greens and ham. Did you know that?"

He hadn't known that, but he supposed there would be many things he and Evaline differed on.

"You should also know that Evaline and I made the pie, but mostly Evaline. She's quite the baker," Frannie added.

Henry figured he knew where this conversation was headed, what with Great-Grandma and her protégé, Frannie, and their "hints".

Finally in an act of bravery, Henry held his breath and took a bite of the collard greens. It took its time sliding down his throat, causing him to nearly retch.

"Would you like seconds?" Great-Grandma asked.

CHAPTER SEVEN

Two weeks later, the rain pattered on the roof five minutes before the Bible club was over for the evening. "Wish we wouldn't have walked," muttered Frannie.

Evaline eyed the olive-green phone on the kitchen counter. "We can always call Dad to come get us."

"I can take you home," Henry offered.

"Thank you," said Evaline. There was no way she was up for battling a rainstorm.

"Sure beats walking," added Frannie.

He opened the church door, then quickly shut it. "It's really coming down out there." Wandering through the church, he made sure everyone else had already left and didn't need a ride as well. Henry then handed Evaline his red-and-black letterman jacket. "Care to borrow this?"

Frannie tossed a sly grin her way. It did look chilly outside, and Evaline still wasn't accustomed to the cooler temperatures in Chokecherry Heights. She rubbed her upper arms with her hands. Couldn't hurt to borrow his jacket, could it? "If you're sure you don't need it."

"I'm sure."

"You should borrow it," offered Frannie, always the number one employee at the peanut gallery.

Henry held the jacket for her as she slipped into it. The long sleeves hung past Evaline's short arms. "Did you participate in sports in high school?" she asked.

"I did. Both basketball and baseball. I wasn't the best on my team by any stretch, but I've always had a love for sports. I'll pull the truck up to the door." He left before Evaline could offer his jacket back.

"Wow, don't you look spiffy," said Frannie. "He's such a gentleman. And to offer you his coat? I think he's sweet on you."

Little sisters were such a pain. "No, he's just being kind. Pastor and Mrs. Gregory raised him right."

Moments later, Henry opened the passenger side door of his truck and Evaline and Frannie climbed in. It was only after she was settled in the seat that Evaline realized she should have chosen to ride shotgun. Especially since Frannie suddenly grew widthwise and took up a whole lot more room than usual. As a matter of fact, Frannie sat as far from the door and as close to Evaline as possible.

Causing Evaline to sit right next to Henry, which was, well, it was awkward.

But not at all bad.

Sitting this close to him, she inhaled the woodsy scent of his cologne. His nearness caused her heart to thrum in her chest.

She argued in her mind with herself about whether Henry might truly be sweet on her, as Frannie said. Not that Frannie was an expert, although she thought she was.

What would she do if her sister's suspicion was true? Especially since they'd only recently met?

Of course, there had been no indication proving Frannie was right, so that meant Frannie was most definitely wrong.

Henry stopped at a stop sign before taking a left turn. At that very moment, he focused his attention on her. His face was so close to hers.

Evaline held her breath. Why did a random thought about kissing enter her mind?

Clearly, she was exhausted. It had been a long day.

"I think you can go now. There's no traffic," quipped Frannie, who at that moment became an expert on motor vehicle travel.

Evaline was so flustered she forgot to return Henry's jacket after he dropped her and Frannie off at home. "You know what that means, don't you?" Frannie asked.

"I'm fairly certain you're going to tell me."

"It means now he has to see you again to get it back."

Evaline shook her head. Frannie was so clueless sometimes. "Of course I'll see him again. Let's see, we go to the same church, work with youth at the same Bible club…"

"Are you counting down the days until church?"

"Frannie, you are completely obnoxious."

"Thank you. That's a compliment." She held a finger to her mouth. "Say, maybe Henry wants to go steady and that's why he gave you his jacket."

Frannie had such a vivid imagination. Maybe she should be a writer. "He loaned me his jacket because it was raining and he's gentlemanly. Nothing else. Besides, I haven't even known him for long."

Evaline walked to the kitchen to get a drink of water. No sense in allowing Frannie to see her blushing cheeks at the comment about Henry wanting to go steady with her.

But there was no getting away from someone who enjoyed playing follow the leader. Evaline nearly bumped into Frannie when she pivoted from the sink.

"Do you like Henry?"

"Ssh. You need to keep it down. Mom and Dad have already gone to bed."

"Well, do you?"

"Do I what?"

Frannie rolled her eyes. "Either your head is always in the clouds, or you're avoiding my question. If it's the latter, your avoiding my question is really giving me an answer to my question."

"You are not making sense at all."

"Sure I am. But let's talk about something else."

That was fine with Evaline. A change of subject was more than welcome. "What would you like to talk about?"

"Do you think Kenny likes me?"

"Sure."

Frannie nearly did a jig right there in the kitchen at 9:05 p.m. If only Evaline had known it would be that easy to redirect the topic from the game of twenty questions.

A few minutes later, Evaline removed Henry's jacket. Making sure Frannie was minding her own business, Evaline took a quick whiff and inhaled the scent of his cologne. She would keep the jacket safe for him until Sunday at church.

But the thought going through Evaline's head as she carefully hung Henry's jacket on the hook in her room was that he might like her.

And oddly enough, she might be okay with that.

***

Henry found he liked having Evaline sit next to him in his truck. That was the second time in so many days. He'd secretly stared at her from the corner of his eye most of the way home. Thankfully there hadn't been much traffic.

The more time he spent with her, the more he liked her. And the more he liked her, the more he wanted to spend time with her.

Sure, she was a quiet one. Sometimes he had to initiate the conversation. But that was okay by him because he found some girls talked way too much. Like her little sister, Frannie, for instance.

Henry hadn't minded that she'd forgotten to give back his jacket. He would see her on Sunday, but hopefully before.

Once inside his house, he tossed his keys on the table. The newspaper, opened to the classified section, beckoned his perusal.

But he already had the contents of the advertisement memorized. He'd attempted to call on the building yesterday, but there was no answer.

Henry needed to try again, but he'd procrastinated. What had him so nervous about inquiring about what could be his future business? Fear? Apprehension? Worry? Concern? All of the above?

The next morning after offering his thousandth prayer for guidance, he attempted to call on the advertisement once again.

After six rings, a man answered.

"Hello? I'm interested in the building you have for sale."

***

Evaline was busy at the library tending to returned books when a familiar face came into view.

"Evaline, can I talk to you for a minute?"

"Ssh," whispered Mrs. Gowrie. "This is a library."

"Sorry, ma'am." Kenny lowered his voice. "So, can I talk to you?"

"Sure. What's wrong?"

Kenny shifted from side to side while simultaneously picking at a fingernail. "It's about Frannie."

Why was she not surprised?

"What about her?

Kenny, a Chokecherry Heights high school football star, a looming presence at six-foot-two, and well over 200 pounds, leaned closer. He folded in half to look

Evaline in the eye. "I haven't let on about this, but I really like Frannie."

"You don't say?" Evaline didn't let on that it was likely everyone in the Bible club, and probably Chokecherry Heights as well, knew of Kenny's affection for Frannie. And vice versa.

"So, here's my dilemma…"

This time, Mrs. Gowrie approached Kenny and tapped him on the shoulder. With pursed lips and a stern expression that removed all trace of pleasantries, she reiterated her favorite word. "Ssh."

When she had Kenny's attention, Mrs. Gowrie continued. "That is the last time I will warn you, young man. This is a library. There will be no vociferous babble on my watch."

"No what?"

"Mrs. Gowrie, with your permission, may I take a short break and meet with our patron just outside the library to address his concern?"

"That would be acceptable, Miss Browning, but do make it expedient."

Evaline nodded. "I will, ma'am." She walked through the swinging door from the front desk area and beckoned Kenny to follow her out the door of the library.

"Where was I?" asked Kenny, as he began to pace. "Oh, yeah. I haven't let on about this, but I really like Frannie. And since you are her older sister, I thought I could ask you a question."

"Go on."

"Do you think she likes me too? I'd really like to know."

Evaline imagined her eyes bulged at Kenny's inquiry. He really had no idea Frannie liked him. When she didn't say anything for a moment, Kenny continued. "Golly, Evaline, you'll tell me won'tcha? I'm a nice young man and all."

"Yes, you are, and in order to remain on my good side, and the good side of my dad, mom, and especially Great-Grandma..." Sure, Frannie could be really annoying at times, but Evaline was fiercely protective of her.

"Great-Grandma? I will for sure want to stay on her good side."

"That is the truth. So you'll need to treat Frannie with respect and vow to protect her with your very being."

It was Kenny's turn to have bulging eyes. "I can promise all that."

"Then in answer to your question, I would say, she may like you, or she may not."

"Aww shucks, Evaline, that's not helpful."

Evaline giggled. "Just prove you're a gentleman and worthy of her, kindhearted, thoughtful, and respectful. Then she has no choice but to like you."

"You mean open the doors for her and buy her flowers, that sort of thing?"

"Exactly."

Kenny puffed out his chest and determination lit his face. "That shouldn't be too difficult. Thank you, Evaline."

He strode off, and Evaline wondered how long it would be before he and Frannie were going steady.

***

"Evaline, may I speak with you for a minute?" Mrs. Gowrie asked as Evaline was about to leave for the day.

She dreaded that it might be about Kenny's interruption today. "Yes, ma'am."

"This is on a lighter topic." Mrs. Gowrie wheeled the book return cart to its rightful place.

Evaline held her breath. What could her co-worker be about to say?

She didn't have to wait long.

"Usually, I'm not a matchmaker in any sense. I prefer to leave things well enough alone. However, I must say it is my full belief that you and Henry would make an extraordinary couple."

This was so far from what Evaline predicted Mrs. Gowrie to say. Her mouth dropped open and the words wouldn't come. Sure, it seemed as though nearly everyone in church, and for sure those in her family, believed she and Henry would make a fine couple, but to hear it from Mrs. Gowrie, the woman who rarely spoke any words other than "ssh" to her?

"You don't have to say anything," said Mrs. Gowrie. "Just know that if I were you, which I'm glad I'm not, but if I were, I wouldn't let that boy get away. Now, hurry and gather your things. I'm closing the library today for Mr. Frankel."

CHAPTER EIGHT

Who knew returning a letterman jacket would bring such embarrassment?

Congregants mulled around the foyer. Finally, she spotted Henry passing out bulletins. For some reason, Evaline was far more nervous around him than usual. She handed him his jacket, then attempted to make a hasty disappearance through the doors to the sanctuary.

"Excuse me," said Mrs. Tidwell, a dramatic woman who made it her mission to keep abreast of all of the happenings in Chokecherry Heights. "I noticed you returning Henry's letterman jacket. You two aren't breaking up, are you? Is that why you are returning it?" She dabbed at her eyes. "You two make such an adorable couple."

Adorable couple?

"Oh, we're not…" Evaline began.

"Don't worry, Mrs. Tidwell," chimed in Frannie, who decided at that moment to make her debut as a reporter for the latest news in the *Letterman Chronicles*.

"Evaline was just returning it because Henry might get cold. Even though it's 75 degrees."

Mrs. Tidwell appeared satisfied with Frannie's response, and Evaline quickly rushed past the woman and into the safety of the sanctuary.

She plopped at the end of the pew, right next to Great-Grandma. Her first mistake.

"I see Henry over there. He just sat down. Do you see him, Evaline? He's in the…" Great-Grandma paused. "The fourth row, third seat. Directly across from you. How convenient."

Evaline surreptitiously peeked at the pew adjacent to hers. Sure enough, Henry sat on the edge, his focus directed toward the front. His handsome profile beckoned her to stare a moment longer.

It was a moment too long, because Henry looked over just then and returned her gaze.

Their eyes locked.

"It's unbecoming of a young lady to stare," whispered Great-Grandma.

Evaline returned her focus to the front of the sanctuary. Mrs. Gregory began to play the piano and everyone stood for the first hymn, "Blessed Assurance". Evaline lifted her voice to the Lord:

This is my story, this is my song,

Praising my Savior all the day long;

This is my story, this is my song,

Praising my Savior all the day long.

She heard Henry's voice as well, clear, strong, and husky. She watched him from her peripheral until again, their eyes connected. Her knees wobbled, as butterflies took up residence in her stomach.

Surely she wasn't falling in love with Henry Gregory.

Or was she?

***

A few days later, Frannie was perched on the front steps of their house when Evaline arrived home from work in the family car. "Evaline? I need to talk to you right away."

"What is it Frannie? Is it Mama, Dad, or Great-Grandma?"

"Pshaw. None of them," said Frannie, waving away Evaline's concern.

"Then what is it?"

Frannie peered in front of her and behind her. "I need to ask you something that must be kept secret between us."

"All right. What is it?" Evaline longed to go inside and have a fresh glass of sweet tea and catch up on the happenings of the day with Mama.

Apparently, with Frannie's never-ending presence, that wouldn't be the case.

"Do you think Kenny likes me?"

Her sister clearly possessed a lack of memory. "Didn't you already ask me this?" And hadn't Evaline recently had a similar conversation with Kenny?

"I am asking you again. Do you think he likes me?"

"Maybe."

"Maybe?" Frannie's eyes grew wide. "Evaline, this is a certifiable emergency. Do you have any information that might ease my frazzled nerves?"

Frannie should go into acting. She'd win an award for sure. "Why are your nerves frazzled?"

"I just…well, I'd like him to like me. I've given hints. Do you think he's caught on?"

"You are an obvious sort of person."

Frannie frowned. "Is that a compliment?"

"Take it as you wish, Frannie. Look, can I go in and get some sweet tea? It was a long day at the library, and I'm famished and likely dehydrated too. It's 105 degrees out here and that's in the shade."

"Maybe you could ask Kenny if he likes me."

Evaline shook her head so hard her overabundant curls swished through the air. "Absolutely not and no can do. I am not a matchmaker, nor will I ever be."

CHAPTER NINE

Several days later, Henry strode into Nathanson's Hardware Store with his list. Mort, Lewis's older brother, waited on him at the counter after he collected his items.

"How are you, Mort?"

"Everything is copacetic. Just working and saving up some money for a car. I've had my eye on that souped-up '57 for sale down at the car lot. It'll beat riding my bicycle everywhere."

Henry knew all about the souped-up '57. He'd eyed it himself.

Mort rang up the items and deposited them into a bag. "Looks like you're gonna be busy today. Say, Henry, Lewis says the Bible club is going well."

"It is. We've grown since we started."

Mort leaned forward on the counter. "So, what do you think of Evaline Browning?"

It wasn't so much *what* he thought of her, but how *regularly* he thought of her, which was far too often. "Why do you ask?"

"She's a swell gal, don't you think? And pretty too."

Henry could count on one hand the times he'd experienced a jolt of envy. This would be one of those times. Did easygoing and jovial Mort have his eye on Evaline? Did she like him too? He did his best to shove aside the dismal thoughts. "Yes, she is a swell gal and pretty too. Smart, as well." That was one thing Henry really liked about Evaline...her intelligence, especially when they spoke on a variety of matters.

Mort squinted at Henry. "You gonna ask her out one of these days?"

"Maybe." What was Mort getting at?

"You sure should. Or I just might." Mort took a step back and crossed his arms across his chest.

Henry sized up his competition. At five-foot-ten on a "tall" day, Henry wasn't considered large. He had broad shoulders and a muscular build, but he was on the leaner side and had never known a chubby day in his life.

Mort, on the other hand, was about six-foot-one, 185 pounds of pure muscle. He was a year younger than Henry, and was a former high school football star. Henry had never played football, but had played basketball and baseball and considered himself a decent runner.

Henry ran a hand through his brown hair that failed to cooperate even when he attempted to put grease in it like the movie stars did. Mort didn't appear to have that problem.

As far as personalities, they both had pleasant ones, but Henry was more laid-back and less boisterous.

Who would Evaline choose if given the choice?

"So, what do you say, Gregory? We could arm wrestle for it. If I win, I ask her out. If you win, you ask her out. I'm not a betting man, but I think I might know who would win."

Henry wasn't a betting man either, but he tended to agree with Mort on his assessment. "You'd probably win on that one, Mort, but I have been thinking about asking her out."

"What's taking you so long? From what I hear—and I hear quite bit working here at my old man's business—everyone thinks you two should go steady. I respect you enough, having gone to school and all with you and you being an upperclassman and preacher man, to not interfere. But just so you know, if you don't ask Evaline Browning out, I will."

Henry pulled the brown bag with his purchases toward him. "I'll ask her out, Mort."

Mort reached over and slugged him on the shoulder. "Attaboy, Hen."

Ten minutes later, after Henry placed the items from Nathanson's in his truck, he decided to stop by Ayer's Diner for a burger. He needed some nourishment after that troubling conversation with Mort.

Henry wasn't shy, but he'd never been exactly bold either. He sighed. If he told Mort he'd ask Evaline out, then he'd keep his word.

Because he was definitely a man of his word.

But what if Evaline said "no"? What if Mort changed his mind and asked her out himself? What if she preferred beefy muscle-men who worked at hardware stores, as opposed to slim guys who were part-time pastors and full-time handymen?

The diner hummed with business and customer voices mingled with the jukebox music. Henry strode along the black and white squared tile to the counter and perched on one of the red swivel stools.

"Henry Gregory, is that you?"

He recognized the voice as one of the women from church and a busybody. He chastised himself for the second classification. Maybe the woman just had a lot to say. About others.

"Yes, it is. How are you, Mrs. Freeman?"

The aroma of hamburgers and fries made Henry's stomach growl.

"Can't complain. I'm eighty-five-years-old, and as spry as ever." She reached up and pinched his cheek, like she'd done ever since he was a little boy. "You're such a nice boy, Henry."

Just like she'd always said for all these years. He wondered if Mom would have agreed with that statement the time he opened a dog orphanage in the house when he was ten. The dogs had chewed on the couch legs and ate everything in sight.

Henry returned his attention to Mrs. Freeman. "Thank you, ma'am."

"You're welcome. Say, I was in the ladies Bible study with Great-Grandma the other day, and she told me some noteworthy news."

Henry braced himself. He could only imagine.

Mrs. Freeman glanced around the diner to see if anyone else was listening. When it appeared she may have some people interested in her conversation, she raised her voice. "Yes, Great-Grandma said you and Evaline would make such a delightful couple. I tend to agree, and so did everyone in the Bible study. As a matter of fact, I was over at the grocery store day before last and Glenda, you know, the clerk who typically works on register three? Well, she said she thought the same thing. She'd done some sort of polling of her customers and the results were impressive." Mrs. Freeman paused. "If I remember correctly, and sometimes I don't, but if I do on this topic, ninety-eight percent of those polled agree that you and Evaline should go steady. In my humble opinion, the two percent either didn't hear the question or were confused. Maybe I should take a poll here."

Henry let out the breath he'd been holding. Sometimes growing up in a small town where everyone knew you and everything about you was not advantageous in the least. "With all respect, Mrs. Freeman, we don't need to take a poll."

"But if you're not convinced…"

Oh, he was convinced all right. Just the episode with Mort set him on the right track.

Mrs. Freeman didn't understand that patience was a virtue, as she continued without allowing him to answer. "As I was saying, if you're not convinced, I can take a poll here, and then another one down at the post office when I mail a letter to my daughter in Missouri. But I do have to say it's right pleasant that Evaline's family moved here. She's such a lovely girl, and Great-Grandma has become one of my most treasured friends."

"They are a fine addition to Chokecherry Heights."

"Yes, yes, they are. Now, take the advice of your elders, Henry, and ask that girl out."

With a mumbled promise to do just that, Henry bid Mrs. Freeman farewell.

Ask Evaline Browning out on a date?

He'd need to spend some serious time in prayer asking for courage.

CHAPTER TEN

♥₀♥₀♥₀♥₀♥₀♥₀♥₀♥₀♥₀♥₀

Henry had certainly been acting peculiar as of late.
"Evaline? Do you have a minute?" he asked in the
parking lot after church services.

"Ooh, I wonder what Henry could want," Frannie
whispered, being her usual nosy self.

Evaline gave her sister "the look" and whispered
back, "Go away, Frannie."

Frannie giggled and bounded off toward her friends.

"Sorry, Henry. I had to make a suggestion to a
certain pesty someone."

Henry laughed, but even that seemed strained. He
stared at her. Come to think of it, he'd done more of
that than usual lately as well. Evaline reached up and
patted her wayward curls. Were they out of place
again?

He continued to stare.

Did she have food in her teeth?

"What is it, Henry?"

It wasn't like him to be overly bashful. But now with his standoffish moment, he made her look like the outgoing one.

Henry gazed around the parking lot. Was he looking for someone?

Mort Nathanson, Lewis's older brother, strutted by just then. "Hello, there, Evaline. Henry." He smiled at Evaline, and she worried he might ask her on a date. Mort had been a tad flirtatious lately. Not that she had anything against him, but although he was friendly and attractive, Evaline would reserve her dates for someone else.

Like maybe the one who stood before her.

Mort finally left and it appeared Evaline might find out what it was that perplexed Henry so. "You're being awfully quiet, Henry. Is everything all right?"

"Yeah. It's…" he scratched his head.

"Is it about someone in the Bible club? Roberta and Ray maybe?"

"No. Everyone's fine, and my dad had a meeting with the elders about the Orlov Family. But no, that's not it."

"Is it your family? Are your parents all right? Your dad preached a convicting sermon, and your mom was her sweet self."

Henry shook his head. "My parents are fine."

"Then what is it?"

"Evaline…"

"Yes?" What had him so nervous?

But Henry said nothing more for a few minutes. This was definitely not like him. "Are you coming down with something?" she asked.

"No, I just…isn't it a pleasant summer day?"

Evaline knitted her brows together. "Yes, it is."

"All right. Well, that's all for now. I'll see you later."

Somehow, by Evaline's way of thinking, Henry had not intended to discuss the weather with her.

***

Why couldn't Henry find the nerve to ask Evaline on a date? They saw each other twice each week, and he talked with her all the time at the Bible club. They prayed together, served together, chatted about the needs of the youth together.

Yet, he couldn't find the courage to ask her on a date.

It's because you're afraid she'll say no, his inner voice taunted.

And because you think she likes Mort.

True, she did offer Mort one of her pretty smiles today in the parking lot at church. Henry recalled in high school how all the girls swooned over Mort. Maybe Evaline did too.

Rejection was tough, and Henry never cared for it much.

Yet, if he didn't ask Evaline out, Mort would.

The following day, Henry met with Dad at Chokecherry Heights National Bank. The day to apply for a loan on the building had come. His parents contributed to the down payment, most of which he'd saved up over several years.

And in a short time, Henry would be the owner of his own business.

Gratitude rippled through him. Only God could have orchestrated such a thing.

***

Each week at the Bible club after the sermon, Henry hosted a challenge. Participants divided into two groups, and Henry called out Bible verses and the students competed to see who could find the verses the fastest, ultimately enabling their team to win. Evaline kept track of the score with tally marks on the chalkboard.

After twelve rounds, Frannie decided to share her thoughts. "Why don't we have a competition between Henry and Evaline?"

Kenny, apparently still trying to win Frannie's heart, agreed. "That sounds peachy keen. Let's you and me be the judges, Frannie."

"And I can keep score," suggested Lewis.

The rest of the youth clapped and nodded in agreement and several someones debated on who might win.

Frannie added again to the conversation. "My vote goes to Evaline. She's super-fast and really knows her Bible."

"I'm going for Henry," said Lewis. "What about you, Kenny?"

Kenny alternated his attention between Frannie and his best friend, Lewis. "Golly, I'm not sure. I guess I would go for…"

Evaline watched as Kenny struggled with the ultimate dilemma. Would he choose the girl he was sweet on or the friend, who, according to Kenny during last week's Bible club meeting, had been his best friend since the late '40s?

"I—uh, I guess I'll choose Evaline."

Frannie cheered and Lewis's brow furrowed. "Some friend you are, Kenny."

"Do we have a say in the matter?" Evaline asked.

Henry patted her arm gently, causing a peculiar tingle to rush from her wrist to her shoulder. "Come on, Evaline, it'll be fun."

Not that she would ever admit it to anyone nor ever voice her opinions to those in the room, especially Frannie, Evaline couldn't deny Henry's handsome smile. "All right. Sure."

Lewis, the self-proclaimed master of ceremonies, made sure Evaline and Henry were seated next to each other at the front table. Frannie, who stood at the podium with Kenny, snickered. Evaline didn't dare wonder what might be running through her mind, but she tossed her annoying little sister a look that told her to keep her thoughts to herself.

It started off rather easy with Frannie calling the first verse, followed by Kenny, and so on. Lewis kept score, which up to this point was tied. The crowd cheered as they each accumulated points, and Evaline's heart raced to keep up with her fingers as they flipped through the pages of her most treasured Book.

"Found it!" she exclaimed when a verse from Nahum was called.

"Got it!" Henry raised his right hand when he'd found the verse in Jude.

"It's down to the wire, folks," announced Lewis, pretending the chalkboard eraser was a microphone. "Ladies and gentleman, the score is tied. Will the winner be the Bible club pastor or will it be the Bible club helper?"

Evaline caught Henry's eye and for a moment he held her gaze. He was a nice-looking man and was kind and...

And she liked him.

A lot.

The verse from Haggai was called, and Evaline scrambled to regain her composure. "Found it!" she squealed. Not waiting for Frannie to call on her, Evaline read the verse aloud.

"Far out, Evaline! You won!" exclaimed Frannie, jumping up and down.

Lewis nudged his thick spectacles higher on the bridge of his nose. "It's highly likely Henry allowed Evaline to win since he's a gentleman."

Evaline wanted to legitimately win. She turned to Henry. "Is that true?"

A smile lit his face.

"Is it?" she asked.

Henry shook his head. "Naw, Evaline, you won fair-and-square."

"I did?"

"Yes."

The thrill of being the winner of the challenge boosted her confidence, but it was soon deflated at

Frannie's next words. "We forgot to say what the winner wins."

Kenny nodded. "Oh, yeah." He whispered to Frannie. "What does she win?"

"Well," said Frannie, that suspicious twinkle in her eye, "Whoever loses has to take the winner to Hayworth's Drive-in Restaurant for dinner and to Johnson's Drugstore and Soda Fountain for a chocolate malt afterwards."

An amused expression crossed Henry's face. "That sounds like a good idea."

Evaline opened her mouth to utter a reply, but nothing came to mind. As if it wasn't bad enough that nearly everyone in Chokecherry Heights had plans to set Evaline and Henry up as a couple, now the Bible club was behind arranging their first date.

CHAPTER ELEVEN

Taking Great-Grandma to her doctor's appointment was an adventure in and of itself. "I really appreciate you taking her," said Mama, hanging up a sheet on the clothesline.

"She will probably want to go to the grocery store afterwards."

"I'm sure she will," agreed Mama. "And we all know that it's not for the faint of heart to take a ninety-year-old shopping."

Evaline knew that full well. She'd done it several times and lived to tell the tale.

"Just remember the 'put it in, take it out plan',," Mama continued.

Evaline reached for a towel and hung it on the line. "I'm not quite as experienced at that as you are." She thought about how the plan to discreetly remove most of the goodies Great-Grandma covertly slipped into the shopping cart would work.

"I've been meaning to ask you how the Bible club is going," said Mama. "Frannie says she's learning a lot and has made several friends."

"One friend in particular named Kenny."

"Oh, yes, Kenny. I've heard all about him."

Evaline laughed. "I'm sure you have. Frannie isn't known for keeping secrets. Something tells me it won't be long before Kenny pays a visit asking Dad if he can take Frannie on a date." She grabbed a clothespin from the basket. If only Henry liked her the way Kenny liked Frannie.

She dismissed the faint tinge of envy. "The club is going well. Henry has a gift for preaching the Word and sharing the Gospel. We had another youth surrender her life to Christ last Wednesday."

Evaline and Mama continued their discussion about the Bible club until Great-Grandma announced it was time to leave.

At the doctor's office, Evaline and Great-Grandma took a seat in the crammed waiting room. Great-Grandma peered around the room through her black-rimmed cat eye glasses. "Looks like it's old people day today," she chortled.

Evaline followed her gaze, noting that nearly everyone was at least two decades younger than Great-Grandma. But then, she'd never thought of herself as elderly.

A nurse opened the door a few moments later. "Great-Grandma?" she called.

Evaline inwardly giggled that in the short amount of time they'd lived in Chokecherry Heights, Great-Grandma had trained nearly everyone she came into contact with on her preferred name.

When she and Frannie someday found their true loves and married and had children, would Great-Grandma have to retrain everyone to call her "Great-Great-Grandma?"

Marriage? Children? Evaline shook her head. Maybe for Frannie. She and Kenny would probably be going steady within a few months. But as for herself, Evaline figured she'd be one of those elderly old maid librarians.

So why then, did Henry's face flash through her mind ever so briefly?

The nurse returned Great-Grandma to the waiting room a short time later. "She had an outstanding checkup," the nurse said. "We'll see you next year about this time unless you have concerns."

"I could have told you I'd have an outstanding checkup," beamed Great-Grandma, who clearly lacked humility. "I'm healthy as a horse. Say, did I ever tell you that we had a lot of horses on our farm back in the day?"

Evaline had heard the story about 400 times, but graciously waited while Great-Grandma shared it with the nurse. When she was finished, the nurse turned her attention to Evaline.

"Great-Grandma was telling me about you and Henry."

Evaline wrinkled her nose. "Me and Henry?"

"I met Henry when he was doing a remodeling project for my husband and me. Such a kind young man. I imagine you two work well in making the Bible club a success.

Why was Evaline not surprised Great-Grandma had been discussing her and Henry?

***

An hour later, they were headed to the grocery store. Great-Grandma rolled down the window and hung her arm out as Evaline drove. "I can't wait to go shopping. It's high time I made some purchases."

Fortunately for Dad's pocketbook, there'd be far less of Great-Grandma's purchases than she was planning.

As they walked into the store, Great-Grandma waved at everyone they passed. She appeared especially spry today in her lime green dress, stockings, and her blue shoes with a homemade flower fringe glued on the top for decoration. She carried her oversized pink knit purse with tassels in one hand and her cane in the other.

Sure enough, as Evaline retrieved the items on Mama's list, Great-Grandma added to the purchases. More than one package of cookies found their way into the cart, and more than one package of cookies found their way back out again when Great-Grandma was otherwise occupied.

In aisle five, Evaline noticed that the can of soup she needed to purchase was on a high shelf. "Goodness, y'all," she moaned, standing on her tiptoes, but still not able to reach it. She hoisted herself on the lower shelf and reached as best she could.

"Wish I could help you, but I can't," said Great-Grandma, likely placing more treats in the shopping cart.

"Just a little higher," Evaline moaned, wishing she'd been born with some height.

Out of nowhere, a hand reached above her head for the soup can. "Is this what you were needing?" a voice asked.

A very familiar voice.

Evaline didn't move. Didn't breathe.

Great-Grandma woke her from her temporary frozen state. "Thank you, Henry. You're such a considerate young man."

Evaline took a step down from the shelf she had climbed on and collided with Henry. Her breath hitched again. Her heart raced in her chest at his nearness. Had she ever stood so close to him?

There were little dark gold flecks in his blue-gray eyes. Couldn't see those from her usual distance. And she was staring right into those eyes. That attractive face. That dimple in his cheek. Those broad shoulders.

She might just forget altogether how to breathe.

"Hi, Evaline."

"Oh, hello, Henry."

A crinkling of a wrapper drew Evaline's attention from Henry. Great-Grandma was eating a cookie from one of the bags. "I'm getting a little peckish standing here waiting forever. A woman could get famished and die of starvation."

***

Evaline pushed the shopping cart to the front of the store, settling on register three, which had less customers waiting in line than register two.

"Oh, Glenda is always so efficient," gushed Great-Grandma. "Come on over to this line, Henry," she beckoned.

Henry shook his head. "I'm fine with register two."

"I'm sorry, everyone, but I'm about ready to go home for the day. Please go to Glenda's line."

"Here's my chance," said Great-Grandma.

"For what?" Evaline asked.

Great-Grandma slipped ahead of Evaline, leaving her to stand with Henry. "To see what flavors of bubble gum they have today. Ooh, my favorite." Great-Grandma grabbed four packages of gum and put them in the cart.

Evaline heard Henry laugh behind her. At least today he seemed less nervous than in the church parking lot a few days ago.

"Well, look who's here," announced Glenda, when it was Evaline's turn at the counter. "How precious that the two of you came shopping together. Did Mrs. Freeman tell you I conducted a poll to see what customers thought of the two of you being a couple?"

"Oh, goodness, y'all," gasped Evaline.

Great-Grandma proceeded to stack the bubble gums on the counter before Evaline could ensure the "put it in, take it out" plan was put into place. She and Glenda then carried on a conversation, leaving Evaline to stand awkwardly with Henry.

"Look, Evaline, could I speak with you for a minute?"

"Sure." Would Henry discuss the weather again?

"I was thinking about how we need to have our date at the drive-in restaurant and a malt at Johnson's Drugstore and Soda Fountain, you know, for the Bible club challenge."

Evaline hadn't forgotten. Her face flushed. Now it was her turn to be nervous. "Yes, we do."

Henry cleared his throat. "May I stop by and ask your dad if I can take you on that date Saturday evening?"

She thought he'd never ask.

Attempting to hear over her loudly thumping heartbeat, she answered, her voice sounding shaky in her ears. "Yes. That would be fine, Henry. Just fine."

CHAPTER TWELVE

♥°♡♥°♥°♥°♡♥°♥°♥♥°♥°♥°

Evaline concerned herself with the thought of Dad speaking with Henry about their date. Maybe she should pray for him. Dad had a witty streak about three miles long.

She ironed her favorite button-up blouse, the one with tiny embroidered lavender flowers and a Peter Pan collar. She pulled on her full plaid skirt and wide belt and clasped her cross necklace around her neck. A pair of clean white bobby socks and her penny loafers would complete her ensemble.

"Are you excited about your date?" asked Frannie, the author of the new book, *550,000 Questions to Ask Your Sister and How to Live to Tell the Tale.*

"Yes." Maybe short, clipped answers would dissuade her.

"Do you think Henry likes you? I mean, you two are going on a date because of the Bible club challenge. Do you think he'd ask you otherwise?"

"Frannie, how am I supposed to know the answer to that question?"

Her sister shrugged. "Just wondering is all. Here, let me style your unruly curls." She stepped toward Evaline, hairbrush in hand. "Have a seat."

Evaline sat on the edge of her hope chest while Frannie touted her beauty parlor skills. After spraying her hair with water, brushing it, and spraying it some more, Frannie took a step back. "I don't want to upset you, but there might not be any hope."

"What?" Evaline panicked. "Henry will be here in exactly ten minutes."

"Well, he may be here in ten minutes, but if you add on Dad's interrogation, you have about two hours before restaurant and soda fountain time."

"Still, I need to be ready."

Frannie sighed. "I've done the best I can. I don't want to say your hair is hopeless, because that's dramatic, and I've never been one for theater, but your hair is, well, hopeless."

"Thank you, Frannie. I'm thankful to have a sister who knows how to make me feel better."

"I believe in honesty."

Evaline shook her head and stood abruptly to peer into the mirror above the dresser. "Frannie! What have you done? I look like a poodle!"

Frannie's gales of laughter did not bode well for the situation.

Laugh or cry? That was the question on everyone's mind. Well, at least on Evaline's mind. Her curls frizzed and expanded far beyond their usual borders. "I won't even be able to make it through the doorway," she whined.

Tears ran down Frannie's face. "Oh, oh, Evaline. You poor, poor dear. Here…here…let me…let me…help you."

"I need no help from the likes of you," she snapped. "You promised to make me look better. Not worse."

A knock at the door caused Evaline to jump. "Henry's here," said Great-Grandma, who then decided to wander through the doorway. "Well, goodness, y'all," she quipped. "Is that a new hairstyle? Some of the fads these days." She removed her glasses, then returned them to her face. "At least you're wearing a spiffy outfit."

After a prayer praying for grace toward Frannie and Great-Grandma and for a miracle for her hair, Evaline set to making herself presentable.

It mattered to her what Henry thought.

***

Henry wiped his sweaty palms on his trousers. *It is just a date. Not a request to seek Evaline's hand in marriage.* He prayed again for courage, a gate over his mouth should he say something ridiculous, and the ability to breathe normally.

Mr. Browning met him at the doorway. "How about a chat in the garage," the older man suggested.

Last time Henry was in the garage, the occasion was a relaxed one. This time that was not the case.

Far from it.

Henry followed Mr. Browning into the garage. "What can I do for you, Henry?"

Was Mr. Browning trying to put him at ease or had no one told him about Henry's reason for a social call?

"I was hoping to take Evaline out for a date to Hayworth's Drive-in Restaurant for dinner, followed by a malt at Johnson's Drugstore and Soda Fountain, sir."

"Ah. Well, Evaline is very important to her mom and me."

Henry nodded as words stuck in his throat.

"Where do you see yourself in five years?"

Five years? Henry just wanted to get through the next five minutes. "Uh, well, I see myself continuing to volunteer at the Bible club. Sharing Christ with teenagers is important to me. And I hope to own my own business. As a matter of fact, I recently went to the bank for a loan on that building over on Fifth Street."

"What kind of business?" Mr. Browning handed him a soda pop. "Here. To calm the nerves."

"Thank you." But Henry doubted the soda pop would calm his nerves. "I hope to have a remodeling business someday. Remodel houses for folks and such."

"Wonderful. It's always advantageous for a man to have a plan. Now, you take good care of Evaline, have her home at a decent hour, and make sure you're a gentleman."

"I will, sir. I promise."

After more discussion, Mr. Browning led Henry back into the house where he waited on the sofa. Three times he caught himself bouncing his knee and instead focused on picking at his fingernail.

Great-Grandma took a seat next to him. "Well, hello there, Henry."

"Hello, Great-Grandma."

"You here for Evaline?"

"Yes, ma'am, I am."

Great-Grandma held her chin high. "I knew all my hard work would pay off."

Evaline arrived a moment later from somewhere in the back of the house. The sight of her took his breath away. Her pretty face, twinkling blue eyes, and her dark blonde curls...

He stood, unable to take his eyes off of her. "You look beautiful."

The way her face lit up at his statement was worth all of the anxiety he'd undergone to take her on their first date.

Had he ever seen anyone so lovely in all his life?

If he wasn't in love with her before, he was now.

Henry hoped she felt the same.

CHAPTER THIRTEEN

My, but wasn't Henry a handsome guy?

Evaline wondered if he could hear her heart beating from his location behind the steering wheel for it was the only thing she could hear.

But goodness, why was she so jittery? Wasn't this the same Henry she assisted at the Bible club? The same one she attended church with? They were friends, so why the nerves?

They ate their meals at Hayworth's Drive-in Restaurant, then headed to Johnson's Drugstore and Soda Fountain. Henry claimed one of the round tables near the back after placing a coin in the jukebox. One of Evaline's favorite songs, a slow and romantic tune, filled the air above the chatter of the customers.

She and Henry were carrying on a pleasant conversation when Barbara from *The Chokecherry Heights Gazette* approached their table, notebook in hand. "Say, this is a momentous occasion. Our readers will be ecstatic that the two of you finally decided to go on a date. May I get a couple quotes?" Without waiting for an answer, Barbara continued. "So how was it that you, Henry, finally decided to ask Evaline on a date? Was it Mort's influence? Glenda's? Great-Grandma's?"

Mort? Evaline wanted to ask what he had to do with the situation.

"It was part of the Bible club challenge," Henry offered.

"Ah, so we can probably thank Frannie, Kenny, Lewis, and the rest of the group?" She wrote furiously in her notebook. "So tell me, do both of you see more dates in your future? Maybe going steady?"

Henry met Evaline's eye. "Evaline Browning, if it's all right with your dad, will you go steady with me?"

"I thought you'd never ask."

"Ooh," squealed Barbara. "May I use that quote?"

***

Later, Henry drove them to the park. "Care for a stroll?" he asked.

She placed her hand through the crook of his arm, and together they meandered through the shaded park.

Mammoth oak trees towered overhead and the scent of flowers lingered on the breeze.

Henry led her to the edge of a pond. Ducks floated on the water, nary a care in the world. "I'm glad we agreed to the Bible club challenge."

"Me too." Would she wake any moment and discover the time spent with Henry was nothing but a fanciful dream?

"Not sure if I told you, but Roberta and Ray's father will be seeking treatment for his alcoholism. The elders and men of our church have rallied behind Mr. Orlov and he has committed to attend regular men's Bible studies. My mom spoke with the Bible study ladies and they are offering full support to Mrs. Orlov. I offered for us to continue to reassure Roberta and Ray that we're here for them."

Evaline was grateful her family found Chokecherry Heights Fellowship. And she was grateful Mama volunteered her to be the Bible club helper.

Henry clasped both of her hands in his. Her breath hitched.

Their gazes locked. "Thank you for agreeing to go steady with me, Evaline. Do you think your dad will give his blessing?" Henry asked, a huskiness in his tone. His nearness caused a fluttering sensation in her stomach. What would it be like for Henry to kiss her?

There was so much she liked about this man. His dedication to the Lord and to the youth at the Bible club, his charming and witty personality, and his handsome appearance. "Yes. I think he will."

A high-pitched voice interrupted the romantic moment between them. "I knew the polls were accurate."

They turned to see Mrs. Freeman standing near them, leaning on her cane. "I came here for a walk with Mr. Freeman," she waved toward an elderly gent leisurely strolling toward them. "He's here to witness this memorable occasion." She beckoned him to hurry his pace.

"Hello, Mrs. Freeman. Mr. Freeman," greeted Henry.

Evaline was disappointed the Freemans had interrupted the moment between her and Henry. "What memorable occasion?" she asked.

"Well, that you and Henry are finally a couple. There has been much arduous and exhausting work to see this event come to fruition, especially with the polls."

"You mean the polls Glenda is taking at the grocery store?"

Mrs. Freeman waved away Evaline's comment. "Pshaw. It's not only Glenda's polls. But all of the extensive surveys the folks around Chokecherry Heights have been taking about whether or not you and Henry will be going steady anytime soon."

Evaline's mouth dropped open. *Extensive* surveys?

Mr. Freeman joined his wife. "It's a nifty turn of events," he said. "Guess you're right again, Mrs. Freeman."

"I'm always right," she quipped.

Mr. Freeman leaned in and planted a kiss on his wife's cheek. "Except when you're wrong."

"There's no need to bring up that one time," muttered Mrs. Freeman. "Now, Henry and Evaline, I'm thrilled beyond words at your decision. This town has been waiting with bated breath for this moment."

CHAPTER FOURTEEN

Six months later

Henry opened the door of the building and he and Evaline stepped inside. *Lord, if it's your will…*

The humble building caused his heart to swell. He could envision the signage on the wall announcing his business. "What do you think?" he asked, expectantly awaiting her response.

She pivoted in a slow circle, her eyes capturing the entire front room. Henry held his breath. Her opinion mattered to him.

A lot.

Finally, she faced him and smiled. "I like it," she said.

Those three words were all he needed. "I would have the office here in this front room, and above the counter there, I'd have a sign." Henry paused and gestured with his arms. "Gregory Home Remodeling". He reached for her hand. "And through these doors is the shop. I'd store all the lumber and my tools in here, all the things

I'd need to refurbish, redesign, and rebuild. No job too small and no job too big. And someday, I'll expand it to building homes as well."

If the front room was impressive, the shop was even more so. "I'll build cabinets and counters and have some samples for customers."

"Oh, Henry, it's perfect. Yes, I can envision your dream of a business in this building."

Henry pulled Evaline into his arms. His lips found hers and he kissed her with longing and passion. Longing for what was to come, passion for the love he'd found with her. And some nervousness because of what he was about to do.

"Evaline," he said, when they parted. "I know we've only gone steady for a short time, and I haven't asked your dad for his blessing yet, and it'll be a while yet before the business is up and running, and…"

"Yes, Henry?"

The lilt in her voice, along with her upturned face nearly made him lose his nerve. He loved this woman. Loved her strong faith; loved her heart for serving others; and loved her spunky personality. He loved her dark blonde curls, her sparkly blue eyes, and her Southern accent. He wanted to spend the rest of his life with her. Wanted her to be his partner in life and in ministry.

He gazed into those twinkling blue eyes and found her lips with his once again. He adored this woman. "Evaline?" he asked before he kissed her a third time.

"Yes."

"Will you…"

"Yes."

"I haven't asked you yet."

Evaline giggled. "My answer to what you're going to ask is 'yes'."

"So, you'll marry me?"

"Yes."

Henry lifted her into his arms. "I love you, Evaline Browning."

"And I love you, Henry Gregory."

EPILOGUE

Present Day

Evaline stared at the photo in the locket. So much time had passed since that first day she met Henry Gregory at the Bible club. They'd shared a lifetime together, although 51 years together was not nearly long enough. She missed him terribly, every day, and every hour of the day.

A knock at the door interrupted her thoughts. Who could be calling at this time of night?

Evaline positioned the locket on the side table alongside her most treasured photographs. She peeked through the peep hole and saw a sight she wouldn't soon forget. Her dear friends, Mrs. Pierce and Miss Bea, stood outside her door in their pajamas. What on earth?

She opened the door. "Is everything all right?"

"Oh, it's perfectly all right." Miss Bea said, her loud voice carrying throughout the halls. She shifted her stance in her pink fuzzy slippers.

"Do come in." Evaline peered down the hall to be sure no one else was out and about at nearly midnight. The halls of the assisted living home appeared quiet and empty.

Mrs. Pierce, dressed in her flowered flannel nightgown, plopped down on the couch and reached up to pat the curlers in her curler-laden gray hair. "We have an idea."

"A lovely idea," added Miss Bea.

"Goodness, but y'all know it's late, right?"

Mrs. Pierce placed her hands in her lap. "Of course, we know. We weren't born yesterday."

"No, it was the day before yesterday," chortled Miss Bea.

Evaline positioned herself in the recliner across from her friends. These two were such crazy old ladies, but they did make life interesting and entertaining. "Do tell. What is your lovely idea?"

"It has to do with your grandson, Quinton, and that girl he 'doesn't' like." Miss Bea popped a mint from Evaline's coffee table into her mouth.

"Irelynn?"

"She's the one," said Mrs. Pierce. "Wait until we tell you our idea."

Evaline clasped her hands together in anticipation. This was the perfect diversion from her lonely thoughts about Henry. "Do tell."

Mrs. Pierce leaned forward. "How do you feel about betting?"

"As in gambling? I don't cotton much to that."

Miss Bea chortled so loudly Evaline feared she'd wake up the neighborhood. "We know your feelings on gambling, Evaline. This is about the consequences Quinton will face if he loses a card game against us."

"How do you know he'll lose?"

A suspicious glint lit Mrs. Pierce's eyes. "Oh, we can manage that. You just follow our lead. And let's just say that if, no when, he loses the card game, he'll be forced to succumb to our matchmaking machinations and take that lovely girl on a date."

Evaline smirked. The more she heard about this idea, the more she liked it. "I'm game, no pun intended."

She couldn't wait for Quinton's next visit.

The boy didn't stand a chance against three matchmaking old gals.

AUTHOR'S NOTE

When I was approached about writing a story about Gram from *Love Under Construction*, the ideas began to flow faster than I could pen them. I knew I wanted to write a novella that could be read alone as a sweet love story or along with *Love Under Construction* as a prequel.

Although *Henry and Evaline* takes place in 1960, for the sake of the story, I took some fictional liberties, while attempting to remain true to the time period. To do so, I reached out to some of my dear older friends, especially those at church. I loved listening to their stories of yesteryear. It was an excellent reminder that we need to get those stories down because once our older friends are gone, so then too, are their stories.

I hope you enjoyed reading about Gram as a young woman. She was a delightful character to write. Or, should I say, "is a delightful character to write"? I have it on good authority that she'll be returning for a visit in my upcoming book *A Love Under Construction Christmas*.

Stay tuned!

ACKNOWLEDGEMENTS

To my husband and daughters, for your continued love and support while I write about my characters and their adventures.

To my dad, for patiently answering my questions about old vehicles, even though you were born in the 1950s and barely old enough to recall the vehicles from that era.

To Judy, for sharing fun stories about your days growing up in a small town in the 1950s and for answering my endless questions. You are such a treasure, and I love your heart for the Lord.

To Wally, for allowing me to borrow your 1958 high school yearbook and for inspiring me with your stories. I love your vibrant personality!

To Gail, thank you for a glimpse into wardrobe styles of the past. Your input was invaluable in shaping Evaline's wardrobe.

To my ACFW writing friends, thank you for sharing clothing details from the '50s and early 60s. I appreciate you all so much.

To my Facebook friends who weighed in on collard greens so I could write an accurate scene for Henry and his experience with a new (to him) food. The general consensus was that collard greens are good, even delicious, if cooked correctly, but are bitter when raw and the windows need to be open while cooking them. Many said they were best served with ham or bacon bits. In Henry's case, (and for the sake of the story), he sided with those who strongly disliked collard greens.

To my readers, may God bless and guide you as you grow in your walk with Him.

And, most importantly, thank you to my Lord and Savior, Jesus Christ. It is my deepest desire to glorify You with my writing and help bring others to a knowledge of Your saving grace.

Let the words of my mouth and the meditation of my heart be acceptable in your sight, O Lord, my rock and my redeemer. ~ Psalm 19:14

ABOUT THE AUTHOR

Penny Zeller is known for her heartfelt stories of faith and her passion to impact lives for Christ through fiction. While she has had a love for writing since childhood, she began her adult writing career penning articles for national and regional publications on a wide variety of topics. Today Penny is a multi-published author of several Christian fiction and nonfiction books. She is also a homeschool mom and a fitness instructor.

When Penny is not dreaming up new characters, she enjoys spending time with her husband and two daughters and camping, hiking, canoeing, reading, running, cycling, gardening, and playing volleyball.

She is represented by Tamela Hancock Murray of the Steve Laube Agency and loves to hear from her readers at her website, www.pennyzeller.com, and her blog, *random thoughts from a day in the life of a wife, mom, and author,* at www.pennyzeller.wordpress.com.

Made in the USA
Middletown, DE
03 March 2022